Grandma's House

Grandma's House

story by Elaine Moore
pictures by Elise Primavera

Lothrop, Lee & Shepard Books · New York

Printed in the United States of America.
First Edition   1 2 3 4 5 6 7 8 9 10

Library of Congress Cataloging in Publication Data

Moore, Elaine.
Grandma's house.
Summary: A little girl spends the summer at her grandmother's
house in the country, a time which they both thoroughly enjoy.
    1. Children's stories, American.   [1. Grandmothers—
Fiction.   2. Country life—Fiction]   I. Primavera, Elise, ill.
II. Title.
PZ7.M7832Gr   1985   [E]   84-11233
ISBN 0-688-04115-9
ISBN 0-688-04116-7 (lib. bdg.)

To my daughters, Devon and Amy,
and my husband, Mike—**E.M.**

To Ann David and Laura Enos, and
to Punch and Paddy—**E.P.**

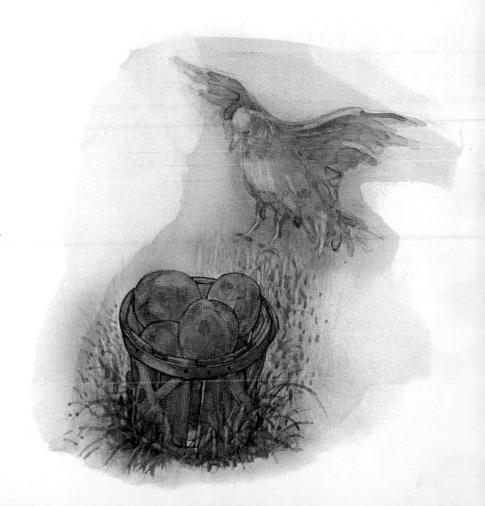

I like summer best because that is when we go to Grandma's house. My mother drives our car there, and the trip takes two days. I sit up front so I can be the first to see the house.

When we finally arrive, my mother parks our car, and I run to where Grandma is waiting.

"Surprise!" I yell, even though I know she has been expecting us.

When Grandma hugs me, she smells of fresh powder. And when she steps back to laugh, it looks to me like her work shirt is laughing too.

My mother can stay at Grandma's for three days. Then she must go home again. Her job is in an office and her boss will miss her, she says. Only I can spend the summer with Grandma.

Every morning, after my mother is gone, Grandma takes me to her porch. She sets a glass of water, a comb, and ribbons on a green wooden table, and stands behind me to plait my hair. I hear her dip the comb into the glass of water. Then she runs it through my hair in a way that doesn't pull or hurt. When the water sprinkles the back of my neck, she smooths the droplets with her fingers. Afterward, Grandma ties a ribbon to the tip of each braid.

One morning, while we are on the porch, I see rabbits in Grandma's garden.

"Look, Grandma!" I shout. "Those rabbits are eating our strawberries!"

I clatter down the steps and wave my arms like two windmills. The rabbits disappear.

Then Grandma leads me to the shed. She takes two buckets off the shelf and hands me the one that has my name on it. Kim.

"Most rabbits don't eat berries," she says. "They eat clover."

"Not your rabbits!" I say, laughing. Grandma laughs too.

We pick the berries, leaving some for the hungry rabbits. The rest we take inside. We slice some to put on top of our cereal. Later, we will make shortcake and strawberry jam.

On the hottest days, Grandma and I go to the mall to cool off. Sometimes while we're there we try on funny hats and make faces in the mirror. Sometimes we go to Chessie's Ice Cream Parlor.

One day, after we've ordered our ice cream, Grandma tells the waiter it's my birthday.

"Grandma!" I say. "My birthday is in December."

"But, Kim," she answers, "I missed your December birthday. You were in school, and I was here. I could only celebrate long distance. I think you should have two birthdays, one at home with your mother and a half birthday in the summer with me."

The waiter must have thought so too, for when he comes with our sundaes, he brings a birthday hat for me. Then everyone in Chessie's sings the birthday song, Grandma loudest of all.

Grandma is right. The next day is sunny. But she is wrong about the birds. They're still eating our peaches.

While Grandma shoos them away, I pull a basket out from the shed. Under the peach tree it is cool and shady and the air heavy and sweet-smelling. We pick the peaches the birds did not touch.

"That's okay, Grandma," I say when I see our basket is only half full. "Peaches aren't my favorite."

"They were last year, Kim," Grandma answers. "You couldn't get enough of them." Then her face brightens. "You just wait until you taste the plums," she says. "They're not ready yet, but when they are, they'll be the best of all."

Grandma has two plum trees. Every day from then on, I count twelve not-ready plums.

"The plums are growing bigger," I tell Grandma.

"They'll be ready soon," Grandma promises. "Too soon."

"Why too soon?" I ask.

Grandma puts her arms
around me. "My plums are
the last fruits of summer,"
she says. "After we pick them,
it will be time for you to leave.
Then I won't see you until
next year."

That night, when I go to sleep, I think how my summer at Grandma's is like her garden. It begins with strawberries and ends with plums. I wish that I never had to leave.

One morning near summer's end, it is late when I wake up. At first I cannot find Grandma. She is not in her bed or in the kitchen either. Then I hear her talking in her outside voice.

I go to the porch where I see her
standing under the oak tree and
peering up into its branches.
Suddenly, I notice a squirrel running
fast through the grass and carrying
something round and red-purple in his
mouth. He races past Grandma and
scampers up into the tree.

"Grandma!" I shout. "The
squirrels are eating our plums!"

For the rest of the morning, Grandma and I do not feel like talking. At noon, we fill a tray with sandwiches, milk, and cookies that we carry outside.

As we eat, I think about Grandma's garden. I know that tomorrow after my mother comes, I will not be with Grandma again until it is strawberry time. I think Grandma knows this too.

Finally Grandma says, "There is only one thing to do, Kim."

"What's that, Grandma?" I ask.

Grandma does not answer right away. Instead, we climb into her truck and drive along a straight road. Then we turn onto one that is bumpy and has sharp turns.

Grandma parks the truck near a large sign, and we climb out. A man with a brown, leathery face tips his cap to us.

Grandma nods hello. "We've shared strawberries with rabbits and peaches with birds," she says to him. "But the plums—why, the squirrels took all of our plums. They didn't leave a one. So I want two more plum trees. Then, next summer, when my granddaughter comes to visit, I'll have two trees for us and two for the squirrels. Soon there should be plums enough for everyone."

The man smiles a tiny smile. We follow him down a shady path where there are pictures tied to every tree. We look for plum trees with fruit that is the darkest purple and the reddest red. After we make our choices, the man loads them in Grandma's truck. Waving, we beep our horn as we drive away.

That night, after supper,
Grandma and I dig two holes.
We put in soft dirt first, then the
trees. We spread the roots in a
circle. Finally we water them
and smooth the dirt all around.

When we are finished, Grandma points to the oak tree. I turn and see the squirrels sitting on their favorite low branch. I can hear their chatter.

"Oh, no, you're not!" Grandma says, shaking her finger. "These trees are my granddaughter's. Next year, you'll have trees of your own!"

Grandma and I laugh. We know it is not the trees that are important. It is Grandma, and it is me.

Afterward, Grandma and I
go inside. We wash up because
we are going to Chessie's.
Tonight it is Grandma's half
birthday, and it is my turn to
sing loudest of all.